Tim

ANIMAL HOMES

By Sharon Elswit
Illustrated by Jennifer Emry Perrott

Allison G. West, Consultant
Education Department, New York Zoological Society

A GOLDEN BOOK · NEW YORK
Western Publishing Company, Inc., Racine, Wisconsin 53404

Contents

Cover: Opossums sometimes live in hollow logs. See page 18.

For Michael,
who builds us beautiful castles.

What Is an Animal Home?

This is an animal home.

gerbils

So is this.

chimney swifts

And this.

lions

Animals live everywhere on earth. They live in many different kinds of homes.

Animals need homes for many reasons. A home makes an animal feel safe from enemies. A home protects an animal in bad weather. A home gives an animal a place to sleep. A home is a place to raise a family.

screech owl

brown bats

flickers

honeybees

skunk

    Some animals find their homes. Some animals build them. Some animals live alone. Some live together.
    Sometimes animals share a place just as people share an apartment building. There are different kinds of animals living in this hollow tree. They come and go at different times and by different paths.

Homes
Above the Ground

Many animals live in trees or other high places. They are safely out of reach of enemies on the ground.

Each night, chimpanzees build nests high up in trees. The nests are made of branches. There the chimpanzees can rest peacefully, far above other animals.

A squirrel makes a nest of sticks and leaves where it lives all summer. The nest is hidden in the branches of a tree. It has a rounded roof to keep out the rain.

Sometimes a squirrel will move into an empty bird's nest. The squirrel will add a roof.

By late autumn, squirrel nests are empty. The squirrels spend the cold months of the year in holes in trees.

weaver ants

tent caterpillars

garden spider

Many other kinds of animals live in trees. Some of these animals spin silk webs or nests for themselves.

Weaver ants sew leaves together to make a house.

Tent-caterpillar moths spin white tents that are homes for their young.

A garden spider lives in a folded leaf near its web. A thread runs from the leaf to the web. When the thread jiggles, the spider leaves the leaf. It hurries to the web to see what is caught there.

Homes That Wasps Build

Some wasps build homes of mud. They find the mud in puddles and near streams. They carry the mud one little ball at a time. They use it to build nests on trees and twigs, or under bridges or porch roofs.

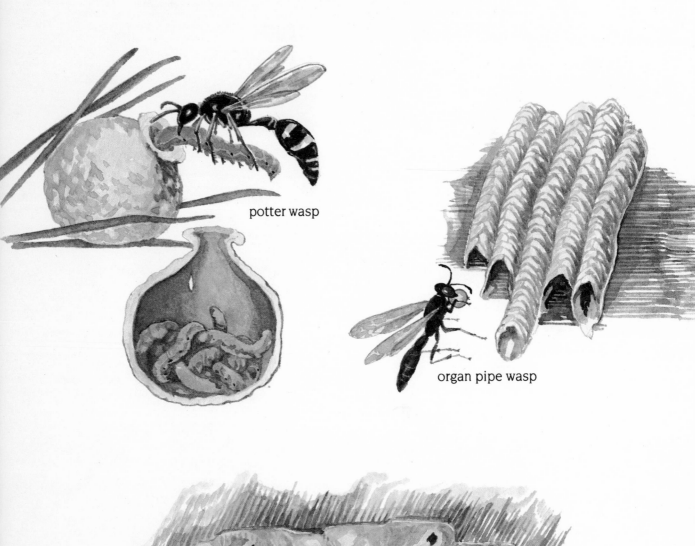

potter wasp

organ pipe wasp

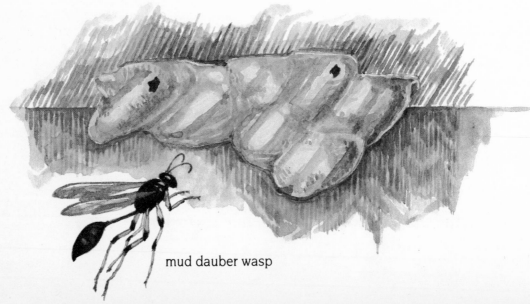

mud dauber wasp

Some wasps build homes of paper. Hornets hang their nests from trees and porches. Yellowjackets build nests in holes in the ground.

Wasps make paper by chewing wood until it is soft. They shape the soft paste into a big hollow ball. It gets hard as it dries.

Each nest has thousands of tiny rooms called cells. A cell holds one wasp egg and some food. Young wasps are hungry when they hatch.

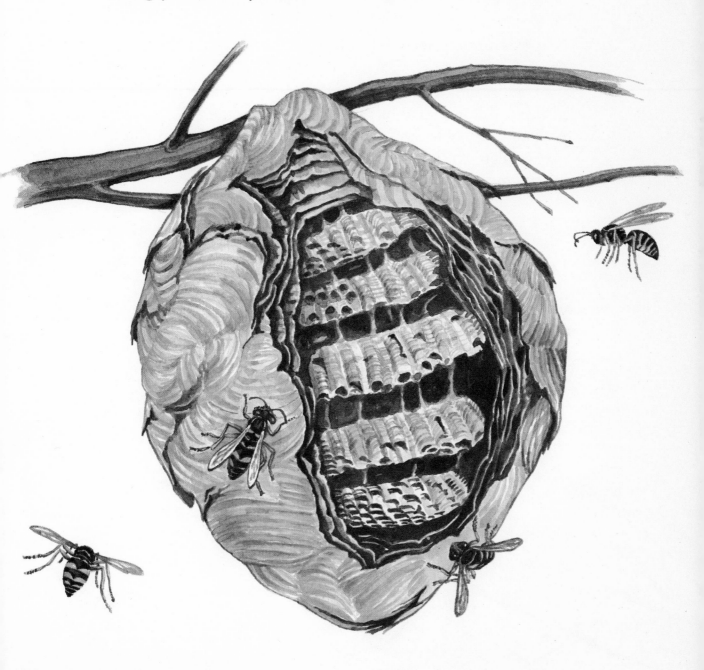

Beehives

Honeybees build homes inside hollow trees. The homes are called hives.

Inside the hives there are many cells. There are cells for sleeping, cells where eggs hatch, and cells for storing food.

The bees build the honeycomb of cells inside their hive from beeswax that they make. The worker bees huddle together to get warm. When the temperature reaches 95 degrees Fahrenheit, flakes of wax come out of the bees' bodies.

The bees make cells by pressing flakes of wax together. Each cell in the hive has six sides.

The queen bee lays her eggs in the hive. The worker bees keep on building around her. When the hive is done, more than 40,000 bees may live in it.

worker bees making cells

worker bees and queen bee

worker bee feeding baby bees

worker bee

Homes That Birds Build

robin

nuthatch

Birds build many kinds of nests in many different kinds of places. The nests hold the birds' eggs and young. Adult birds may sleep in their nests after the young birds have flown away.

Many baby birds—such as robins and eagles—are helpless when they are born. They must stay in their nests until they learn how to fly. That is why the nests must be strong and safe, built up high in trees or on rock walls.

All birds do not build their own nests. Some steal moss and sticks from other birds' nests. Starlings may take over a nest by chasing the other birds away.

Nuthatches sometimes steal nests from starlings. Nuthatches are smaller than starlings. They close part of the entrance to the starling nests. The bigger birds cannot fit inside.

Hummingbird

The tiny hummingbird builds a nest that is less than one inch around. The nest is made from spider webs and very thin plant fibers.

Bald Eagle

Big bald eagles build huge nests. They use sticks and tree branches five feet long. Each year the eagles make their nests bigger. When an eagle nest gets to be too big for its tree, the tree falls down.

The largest nest ever found was in Vermillion, Ohio. Eagle families used it for 35 years. It weighed two tons.

Sociable Weaverbird

Sociable weaverbirds use 10 or more different kinds of loops and knots to make their grass nests. As many as 100 birds may live under one roof.

Northern Oriole

A father northern oriole helps a mother to find plant fibers, hair, and bark. Then he sits nearby and sings while the mother weaves the nest. In 12 days the nest is finished. It swings like a cradle in the wind.

Swiftlet

Swiftlets make nests from their own saliva. They build their nests in caves. In China, people collect the nests and use them to make soup.

Woodpecker

A woodpecker taps a hole into a hard tree trunk with its strong beak. The hole is just as big as the woodpecker. Then the woodpecker hollows out a room big enough for four or five baby birds.

Cliff Swallow

Cliff swallows use small bits of mud or clay to build their nests. The clay bakes in the sun and gets hard. The finished nests look as if they were made of many little bricks.

Homes
On the Ground

Many animals move into natural shelters instead of building homes.

A cave can be an animal's home. A wolf, a cougar, a bear, or a porcupine might live inside.

A hollow log can make a snug house for a skunk, a lynx, a wolverine, an opossum, or a weasel.

A copperhead snake might live in a rotting woodpile. A rattlesnake might just curl up under some rocks.

cougar

weasel

copperhead snake

A female black bear sometimes makes a winter home just by leaning against a tree or a rock.

Snow drifts over her until she is buried.

The snow close to her body melts, making a little snow cave with room inside for the bear and her cubs.

Many animals need better homes than they can find. They build homes to keep themselves and their children dry and comfortable and safe.

Wood rats made this home in a thicket. It looks like a pile of twigs, but it has five rooms inside. Rat houses like this one can reach as high as six feet.

Some wood rats live in the desert. They make a fence of sharp cactus spines to keep coyotes away.

The tallest houses on the ground are built by termites in Africa and Australia. The termites build towers more than 20 feet high.

The towers are made of dirt and saliva. They have a hard outer crust.

Inside the towers, the termites dig tunnels and rooms. The tunnels begin under the ground and may reach all the way to the top of the tower.

A termite queen and thousands of workers live in each tower. There is room for the queen's eggs, too.

termite workers

termite queen

Home Ranges

An animal may live in one special area called a home range. In this area, there are places where the animal always goes to rest. The animal knows the best places to win fights on this land, and the best places to hide.

Animals almost never leave their home ranges. A home range can be the area around an animal's house. For animals without houses, the home range is like a house without walls. Inside it, the animal can find everything it needs to live from day to day.

Home ranges are different sizes. Otters need 200 square miles to move around in. A deer may need only half a square mile.

Most animals must share part of their home range with other animals. They leave signs to warn others that a place is theirs. Giant pandas make scratches on trees and leave a smell on the ground.

otters

deer

giant pandas

Homes Under the Ground

Burrows are homes that animals dig under the ground. They are called warrens for rabbits, dens for foxes, and setts for badgers. Many other kinds of animals live in burrows, too.

Simple burrows have a tunnel that goes down into the ground, a nest for sleeping, and a pantry for storing food. There may be rooms used as toilets. Drains may carry rainwater away from bedrooms. There are usually back doors for escaping from dangerous visitors.

coyote pups

Most burrows go down only two or three feet. But ants dig tunnels as deep as 15 feet.

A chipmunk burrow is not much more than one foot deep. But the shallow burrow still makes a cozy home.

An animal may try to move into an empty burrow instead of digging a new one. This woodland burrow was home for three different animal families in three years. Each family changed the burrow a little to meet its needs.

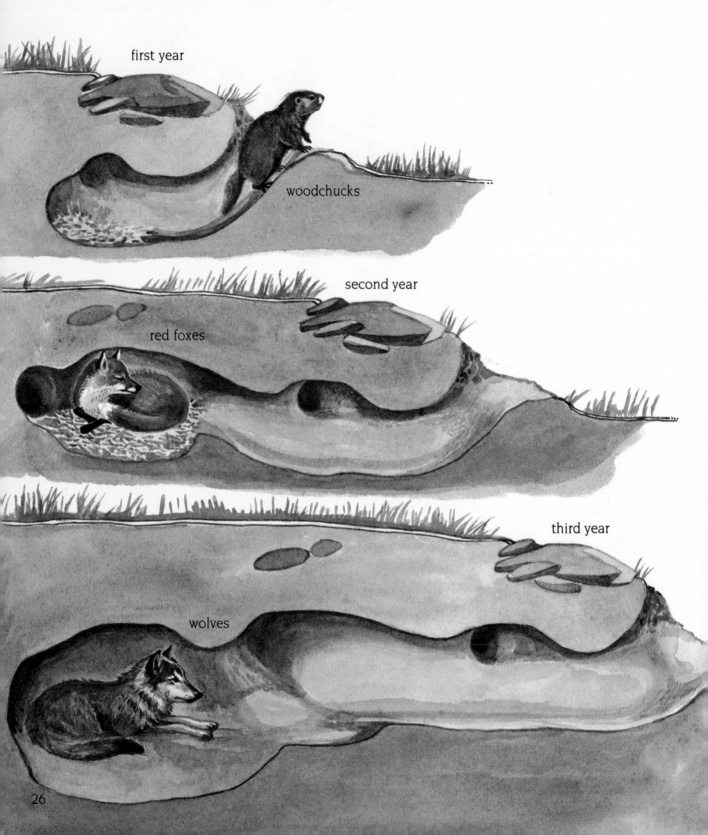

first year

woodchucks

second year

red foxes

third year

wolves

How a Mole Digs Its Home

Moles spend most of their lives underground. They are expert diggers. In one hour, a mole can dig a tunnel 13 feet long. To turn around, the mole must flip over.

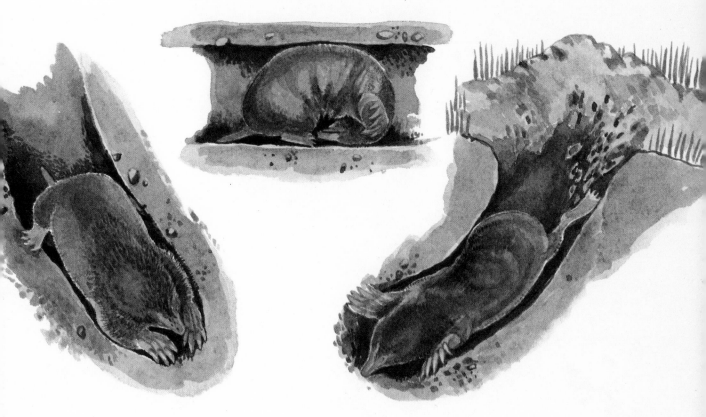

One of the smallest burrows is made by the trap-door spider. Its burrow is only a few inches long. The spider makes a silk door to cover the opening. It hides the door with sand. It can hold the door closed when enemies try to get in. And it can spring the door open to surprise and catch insects for food.

Prairie Dog Town

Prairie dogs live in burrows, too. Prairie dog families connect their burrows until they make whole towns. These towns can be larger than 50 football fields put together. They can hold thousands of prairie dogs.

When the prairie dogs stop using a tunnel, another animal may move in. A rattlesnake or a burrowing owl may live in an empty prairie dog tunnel.

mound

guard room

nursery

nest

Homes
In the Water

staghorn coral

brain coral

clown fish

sea anemone

sea fan

moray eel

starfish

A part of an ocean or a whole lake or pond can be an animal's home.

A coral reef is a good home for sea animals that like to live where the ocean is warm. As many as 3,000 different kinds of animals may live in a large coral reef.

Some animals hide in holes and caves in the reef. They may wait to catch fish that swim by. Some animals look like reef plants or parts of the coral. It is hard for their enemies to find them. And they can surprise other fish they want to eat.

Coral is formed by millions of tiny animals that cling together. A reef is the pile of skeletons they leave when they die.

The most famous coral reef is the Great Barrier Reef off the coast of Australia. It is more than 1,000 miles long.

flamingos

water spider

grebes

Some animals live in the water in marshes. Marsh animals use plants and dirt to build homes.

Flamingos scoop up mounds of mud to make their nests. The top of the mound is shaped like a cup so that the egg will not fall out.

Grebes build nests that float like rafts. They tie the nests to water plants.

Water spiders live in balloons they weave for themselves. They attach the balloons to underwater plants. They keep the balloons filled with air so they can breathe.

Javanese flying frog

sticklebacks

Most fish and frogs lay their eggs right in the water. But there are also fish and frogs that build sturdy homes in ponds and lakes.

A father stickleback weaves a hollow basket out of water plants. His children will be born inside. He cements the tiny home to the bottom of the pond.

Javanese flying frogs hang a foamy ball of mucus from a branch that hangs over a pond. Inside the ball, their tadpoles can swim around. The first heavy rain washes the tadpoles into the pond below.

A caddisworm makes its home of sand or pebbles or twigs, all held together by silk the caddisworm spins. The caddisworm crawls around with its home on its back. When the caddisworm becomes a fly, it leaves its nest at the bottom of the lake.

caddisworms

Beavers build strong houses in the w[...]
family helps to get the job done.

The beavers cut down whole trees [...]
teeth.

They move the logs downstream. [...]

They build a dam with logs and m[...]

The dam holds back the water t[...]
beavers build their house in this pon[...]

air hole

bed

entrance

storeroom

A beaver house is a round lodge made of sticks and mud.
The mud holds the sticks together. Mud also makes the
lodge strong and waterproof. Inside, beaver kits share a soft
bed of fluffy shredded wood.

The biggest beaver dam ever found was 4,000 feet long. It
was built in Berlin, New Hampshire. Beavers made 40
lodges in the pond over the years.

Animal Homes and People

People have changed the way animals live.

People have built cities where there used to be fields and forests. Animals such as wolves are forced to live in a few small wilderness areas.

People hunt animals. People pollute the land and water that animals need to live.

People have also set aside some safe places for animals. These places are called preserves. In preserves, wild animals can live as they always have.

Some animals have moved in with people—even when people didn't invite them.

Cities are full of animal life.

City animals have learned to use what they find. Mice nest in building walls and old mattresses. Rats move into basements.

City birds build nests on the outsides of buildings. Starlings weave strips of newspaper into their nests. Sparrows collect string and gum wrappers for their nests.

Cockroaches have lived on earth for 350 million years. These days they make city homes in warm electronic equipment and other places.

rats

PIZZA

mice

sparrows

cockroaches

starlings

People keep cats and dogs as pets. These animals share their owners' homes and food.

But when people stop taking care of their pets, the animals must take care of themselves.

Stray cats run wild in cities. They usually live alone. They can find food in alleys and they can squeeze into tight places for shelter.

Dogs like to hunt and travel in packs. A pack of stray dogs is easy to spot. Stray dogs are caught by dogcatchers and taken to animal shelters.

Animal Homes
That People Build

Many animals live in houses that people build just for them. Some special homes that people make for animals are:

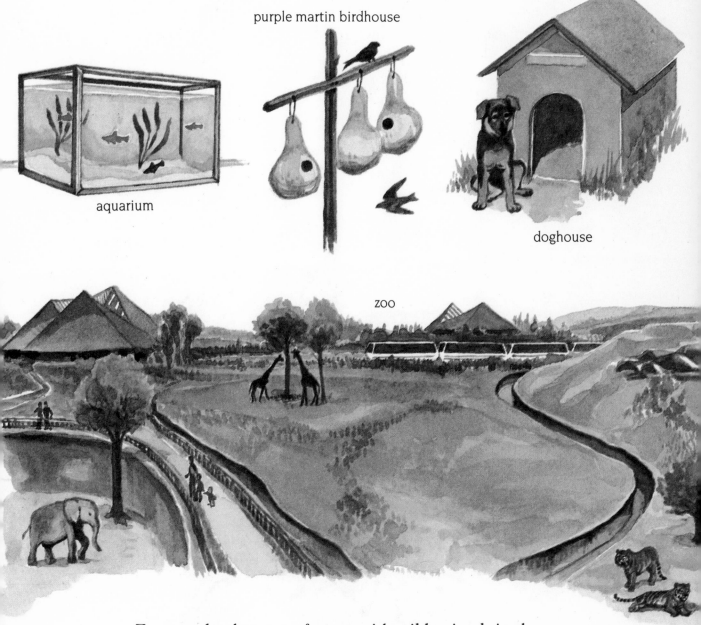

purple martin birdhouse

aquarium

doghouse

zoo

Zoos used to be rows of cages with wild animals in them. But the animals did not live long and healthy lives in zoos. Now zoo planners try to copy the homes the animals would make for themselves.

A Dangerous World

The lives of animals are full of danger. Lightning may set fire to the trees where animals live. Bad weather may kill the plants they eat. Enemies may try to eat them.

But each animal knows the best kind of home to keep itself and its children safe. Animals also know the best places to make their homes. A soldier crab is comfortable burrowing into sand. It can dig its shallow burrow quickly when an enemy attacks.

A prairie dog's tunnels would collapse
in soft ground. The prairie dog must dig
in harder ground. It needs deep, sturdy
tunnels to escape from its enemies.

Nests, burrows, caves, or holes in trees,
animal homes are special safe places in
this dangerous world.

Other Books About Animal Homes

Cartwright, Sally. ANIMAL HOMES. Pictures by Ben Stahl. Coward, McCann, 1973.

Gans, Roma. IT'S NESTING TIME. A Let's-Read-and-Find-Out Book. Pictures by Kazue Mizumura. Thomas Y. Crowell, 1964.

McClung, Robert N. ANIMALS THAT BUILD THEIR HOMES. Books for Young Explorers. Color photographs. National Geographic Society, 1976. This book is available from the National Geographic Society as part of Set V, #00205.

About the Author and Artist

Sharon Elswit spent eight years teaching high school and university level courses, and six years as a children's librarian. She has written stories, poems, and articles, and she is the co-author of computer scripts for use in junior high schools. Ms. Elswit lives with her husband and young daughter in New York City.

Jennifer Emry Perrott studied art at Pratt Institute in New York City, and later worked at the American Museum of Natural History. She has done illustrations for the Smithsonian Institution and Readers Digest. Ms. Perrott lives in Arlington, Virginia, with her husband and two children.

Index